Disney

# WISH

# WELCOME TO ROSAS!

By Steve Behling

Illustrated by the Disney Storybook Art Team

A Random House PICTUREBACK® Book

Random House 🏠 New York

rhcbooks.com
ISBN 978-0-7364-4206-0 (trade)
Printed in the United States of America
10 9 8 7 6 5 4 3 2 1

# ¡Hola! Shalom! Salam!

My name is **Asha**, and this adorable, pajama-wearing goat is **Valentino**. We welcome you to **Rosas**, a **magical kingdom** where wishes actually do come true! How is that possible, you ask? I'll tell you!

Everyone in Rosas has **a wish deep in their heart.** What do you dream about? Maybe you want to climb the highest mountain. Or you might want to be the best dressmaker in all the land. The great sorcerer, **King Magnifico,** grants one lucky person's wish at a monthly ceremony. Whatever the wish, it's bound to come true in Rosas. Because **anything is possible** in the Kingdom of Wishes!

Now I invite you to join Valentino and me on a **tour of Rosas!** I know what you're thinking: "Who *is* this Asha person? And why is *she* giving the tour?" I'm so glad you asked! It just so happens that I'm a **tour guide.** That's right—I am an expert in all things Rosas, *and* I love showing **new friends** around!

But this is no ordinary tour. Get ready for a **special experience.** Because Valentino and I will show you sights that **very few people** ever get to see—places that are usually for King Magnifico's eyes only!

So step this way and stay close—you don't want to get lost, do you? We'll take you to our first stop: **the castle,** where King Magnifico and Queen Amaya live!

Okay, you probably didn't think a tour of the castle would start in the **kitchen**, right? Well, this place means a lot to me, and not just because **delicious treats** come out of its ovens. It's because the person who bakes them is **my best friend, Dahlia!** Not only is she a pastry genius, but she's kind and funny and I can depend on her for anything!

Dahlia can't run the kitchen alone, though. She's just a teenager, like me!

A group of friends helps her prepare the royal meals. There's Hal, who brings sunshine into every room she enters. Simon is an expert napper— he can fall asleep anywhere! Safi is allergic to everything, even his beloved chickens. Gabo is grouchy, but don't take it personally. Bazeema is so quiet you wouldn't hear her come right up behind you! And finally, Dario is a goofball with a heart of gold.

Dahlia and her friends have meals to serve, so let's move on to the area of the castle where the king and queen carry out their **royal duties**.

Please **watch your step!** I remember the sense of wonder I felt the first time I walked up this grand staircase with **Queen Amaya**. The castle is beautiful, and there's so much to see!

Step right this way, and we'll take you inside a **very special place** that only special people (like you!) get to see: King Magnifico's study, where he keeps his books about magic. There's a book focused on fire magic and another that contains a complete history of spells! There's also an ancient book of forbidden magic encased in glass . . . but **don't touch** that one! It's dangerous.

Are you ready to see the most **secret room** in the castle—and all of Rosas? Valentino and I present to you . . . King Magnifico's **wish chamber!** You're very lucky, since no one—I mean *no one*—is allowed in here! That's because in this very room the king **keeps the wishes** that belong to the people of Rosas.

The first time I was in here, King Magnifico himself showed me the wishes. Each bubble contains a single **joyous wish** as beautiful as the person who wished it! King Magnifico told me that it was his duty to **protect the wishes**, no matter what. I wanted to protect them, too.

Shhh.... Did you hear footsteps? We'd better get out of here. You see, there's something you should know.... **Can you keep a secret?**

I recently learned that King Magnifico has no intention of granting every wish. He thinks some wishes are **dangerous**. In fact, he will only grant a wish if he believes it will be good for Rosas. And the king will stop at nothing—including using **forbidden magic**—to keep the wishes under his control.

But I believe that **every wish** deserves the chance to come true. Don't you? I thought so. Now, quickly, let's go before someone sees us!

Whew, that was close! But don't worry, we're safe here. This special place is **the wishing tree**. My father used to bring me here to dream when I was a little girl. He said the stars are there to **guide and inspire us**. They remind us that anything is possible!

The other reason I wanted to take you here is because it's the place where, not too long ago, I made a **special wish** on a bright, **twinkling star** in the sky. And this wish of mine? Well, it would change my life—and Rosas—forever.

What's that? You want to know about the wish I made? Of course you do. I simply wished for the people of Rosas to have the chance to **make their own dreams come true**. Now, follow me!

Oh, good, we're here! Remember that star I wished upon? Well, this **clearing in the woods** is where I first saw it up close! That's right, Star is a real, honest-to-goodness **wishing star** that came down from the sky to help me make my wish come true.

Now, if you'll just turn the page, we can continue our tour and—

*Maaa!* Pardon me, Asha. I'm sorry to butt in, but I've got **a lot to say!**

Hello, everyone! As you know, my name is **Valentino**, and yes, I'm a goat. **A *talking* goat!** Star sprinkled me with stardust, and voilà—now I have this **gorgeous voice!** Star gave voices to the bunnies, squirrels, and bears, too. How ***maaarvelous*** is that?

While we're on the delightful subject of **talking animals**, I must tell you that Asha forgot to show you perhaps the single **most *maaagical* place** in all of Rosas! Not to worry. I, Valentino, promise to make up for this em*baaa*rrassing oversight.

**Now, hold on to your pajamas.** With my *maaagnificent* voice leading the way, I will take you to a realm of **enchanted, everlasting wonder!** (Drumroll, please . . .)

Behold . . . the chicken room! I know what you're thinking: a room full of chickens must be loud and stinky—and not necessarily in that order. That's what I thought the first time I visited. But when Star and I combine our talents, these squawking, egg-laying beauties become a *baaand* of sweet-sounding songbirds. Their wings can't fly, but their voices can!

Now, take a seat, and I will treat you to the performaaance of a lifetime. And a-one and a-two and—

Excuse me, Valentino? The chicken room is very . . . uh, impressive? Is that the right word? And I'm sure everyone would love to hear the chickens sing, but we're running out of time for our tour—and there's still one more spot we need to show our guests. It's the most important place in all of Rosas. . . .

This is **my home**, where my family lives. Meet my mother, **Sakina**, and my grandfather **Sabino**. They are the **most special people** in my life and helped make me the person I am today. I would do anything for them, and they would do the same for me.

Home is also special for me
because it's where Sakina gave me
these **dashing pajamaaas!**

Sadly, we have come to the end of our tour. It's time to say goodbye—unless, of course, you want to stick around Rosas a little longer! Remember, I wished for the chance to make your wishes come true. So all you have to do is wish for the tour to continue, and then turn to the beginning of this book. Valentino and I will see you there!